The Field Mouse
AND THE
Dinosaur Named Sue

The Field Museum

STONE HOUSE
PRODUCTIONS, LLC

SCHOLASTIC

To Richard and Lina Hazle

With special thanks to
JOAN CARRIS, CHERYL CARLESIMO,
SHARON SULLIVAN, AMY LOUIS,
and KIMBERLY WEINBERGER
—J.W.

For my wife, Stevie, with love
—B.D.

With thanks to Jean Carton

Copyright © 2000 by The Field Museum.

All rights reserved. Published by Scholastic Inc.
SCHOLASTIC and associated logos are trademarks and/or registered trademarks of Scholastic Inc.
SUE and the SUE logo are trademarks of The Field Museum.

Photography credit: page 32: The Field Museum, Neg# GEO86160-3c, photograph by John Weinstein.

Library of Congress Cataloging-in-Publication Data available

ISBN 0-439-09984-6

12 11 10 9 8   09

Printed in Mexico   49
First printing, April 2000

SCHOLASTIC INC. AND THE FIELD MUSEUM PRESENT

The Field Mouse
AND THE
Dinosaur Named Sue

BY JAN WAHL • ILLUSTRATED BY BOB DOUCET

SCHOLASTIC INC.

New York   Toronto   London   Auckland   Sydney
Mexico City   New Delhi   Hong Kong

Early one morning, Field Mouse heard strange noises outside his burrow. Some loud, some soft.

SCRITCH! SCRATCH! CHIP! And BANG!

His house had a roof made of an old bone. Field Mouse peered into the hot day. People with shovels, scrapers, and picks dug into the bluff above. Carefully. Slowly.

"Oh my!" cried a young woman. "Look at this *beautiful thing!*"

She showed the others a bone like his roof. Old bones lay all over the place. They were no good for chewing on. They were like rock. In fact, they *were* rock.

That day — and the next and next and next — diggers kept digging. Field Mouse had to see what was happening. In the afternoon, he wished to take a nap.

He scurried back to the home he had known his whole life.

When he got there, he saw a terrible sight. His burrow was torn open—the roof was gone! *They took my bone away. Now I must find it,* he decided.

Packing boxes lay here and there. Old, old, old bones were wrapped in burlap and placed gently in wooden boxes.

A worker put a cheese sandwich down on the edge of a box. The cheese sandwich fell in.

Field Mouse thought his bone might just be in that box, too. He climbed in. He sniffed and poked.

But he could not find his roof.

Suddenly a lid was put on the box. It grew black as pitch.

The box was lifted onto a truck and the truck drove off.

At first Field Mouse lay on the sandwich.

His stomach rumbled from hunger. It kept him awake. The cheese smelled wonderful. *Well,* he decided, *I'll try eating this.* It *was* wonderful.

But he missed his home.

The box was taken to a place called Chicago where they had a huge building. The building was called The Field Museum.

The box was put on a shelf in a cool place in a special room.

One morning, the lid on the box was opened.
Field Mouse jumped out. On tables lay more bits and
pieces of old bones. Some large. Some tiny.

A man was studying them and didn't see him.
Field Mouse looked and looked for his roof.

He flicked his tail and ran when he heard voices.

"*Sue* mumble mumble," said one.

"*Sue* mumble," said another.

What is Sue? wondered the mouse.

He squeezed through an opening in the wall and out of the room.

He scampered up onto a ledge,
searching for his bone. He saw something
so tall it reached to the sky of the hall.

It was Field Mouse's first dinosaur.
It had no skin or fur! Down below him,
people gazed at the critter. They were
small as insects.

He grew dizzy and felt lost.

Field Mouse hid until nighttime. Then he crawled up to a window. Beyond, many lights of the city twinkled.

Far off was a lake. It made him thirsty. He found water in a plastic cup someone left on the floor. He tipped it over and drank.

When visitors were gone, Field Mouse was free to run.
He saw colors through another glass window.

He didn't know it, but he was looking at Chicago as it
was — 410 million years ago.

There were plants. Corals. Snails and shells.
He scratched to get in.

Field Mouse soon grew tired and pushed himself into a small space in the wall. There it was dark and he could close his eyes and remember home.

When he awoke, he saw a man polishing the floor with a machine that whirred loudly and spun.

Field Mouse almost got pulled into it! He wiggled and jumped. He raced down the length of the hall and passed two elephants. He ran and ran until his legs wouldn't go anymore. Then he collapsed in a corner and fell asleep.

In daytime, if no visitors were near, Field Mouse crawled up and peered into a special place where people seemed very, very busy.

They scraped at bones big and little. Or poured plaster on others. They were as careful as the diggers who found the bones had been.

They looked odd — because they wore masks. Dust flew in the air as they took tiny stones away from old bones.

There was a lot to explore. Every room was different. And he found more people working on bones. Maybe one bone was his roof? He kept searching.

Mostly, Field Mouse hid behind walls. It was best
to come out only at night.
He learned to tunnel from one room into another,
squeezing into the tiniest crack.

One day, he entered a great, high room with plants big as trees. Giant dragonflies big as birds. This was Chicago — 300 million years ago.

He sniffed and sniffed. Nothing was real, nothing to nibble on. He missed his home!

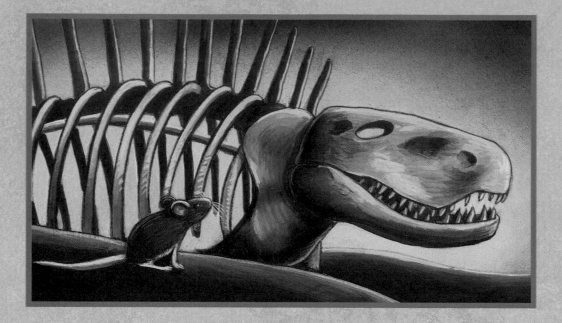

Field Mouse felt he would never find his bone.
There were so many strange creatures all around him.
He liked to look at DIMETRODON. The eyes
were empty holes but seemed to stare at him.

He began to explore APATOSAURUS. Its tail
alone was thirty feet. The critters became his friends.
They had so many bones.

Field Mouse thought TRICERATOPS was scary.
Did these critters have fur like him? Were they lizards?
Field Mouse found it was fun to climb up their backs
and slide down to the floor.

He took naps where he could, but wished he had
a cozy spot of his own.

One day, to his surprise, the giant critter in the great hall was gone. Men and women kept going back and forth. They were putting up something to keep the crowds away.

Field Mouse still had not found a home. To cheer himself up he went to the cafe. He found a scrap of tasty, excellent cake.

He was hearing "*Sue* this." "*Sue* that." His ears rang with "*Sue*." What was it?

Then, one morning, there it was.
All put together. The Sue they talked about.
The biggest T. rex in the world!

She was 67 million years old. Of course he didn't know that. A lot of people stood in front, admiring her.

She had peculiar short, stubby arms. *Poor thing,* thought Field Mouse. *How did she ever pick up a piece of cheese?*

Later that night the hall lay empty. Except for Sue and Field Mouse.

He walked up to each foot. He climbed on her toes and crawled up a leg.

Slowly he climbed up, searching.

In coming down, he stopped in the middle of the other foot. His bone! *His very own bone!* He chattered to Sue. She kept silent.

Under his bone it was dark and cool and safe. A fine place for a secret nest. He made it with bits of paper. Smooth and round.

Maybe Sue had been a terrible, angry hunter — once. Crashing through forests of tall magnolia or oak trees. But now she was quiet and gentle.

Field Mouse was sure she was singing a soft song. Under the foot he dreamed a happy dream.

He was home.

The True Story of SUE

Found in the dry, rolling hills of South Dakota, SUE has captured the imagination of people the world over. Declared the largest and most complete Tyrannosaurus rex ever found, SUE's immense size and near-perfect condition make her nothing less than the find of the century.

Her story began in 1990, when a fossil hunter named Sue Hendrickson happened upon some bones jutting out of a cliff. After SUE's bones were painstakingly removed from their rocky resting place, a journey began which lasted several years. In 1997, SUE's new home was announced: The Field Museum of Chicago.

The knowledge scientists at The Field Museum and around the world will gain from SUE in the decades to come cannot be measured. Unveiled to the public in the spring of 2000, SUE stands tall once again — a breathtaking testament to a long ago time when these powerful and mysterious creatures roamed the earth.